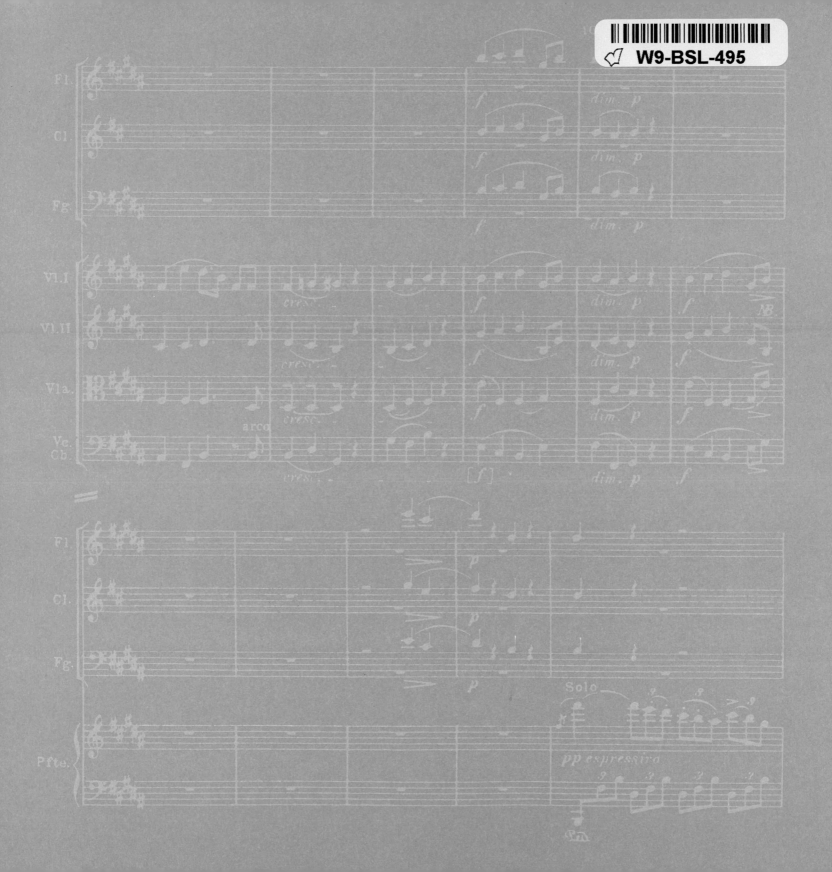

The Living Clarinet

BY BARRIE CARSON TURNER

Alfred A. Knopf  New York

THIS IS A BORZOI BOOK PUBLISHED BY ALFRED A. KNOPF, INC.

Text copyright © 1996 by Macmillan Children's Books. CD Sound

Recording (MACCOM 3) copyright © 1996 by EMI Records Ltd.

Picture credits appear on page 47. All other illustrations

copyright © 1996 by Macmillan Children's Books, London.

Printed in Singapore

ISBN 0-679-88179-4

10 9 8 7 6 5 4 3 2 1

Contents

Overture	5
The Clarinet Family	6
Wind Instruments Around the World	8
Instrumental Groups	10
The History of the Clarinet	12
How the Clarinet Works	16
How the Clarinet Is Made	18
How the Clarinet Is Played	20
Mozart	22
Beethoven	24
Crusell	26
Spohr	28
Weber	30
Rossini	32
Mendelssohn	34
Schumann	36
Brahms	38
Reger	40
Great Players	42
CD Track Listings	46
Acknowledgments	47
Index	48

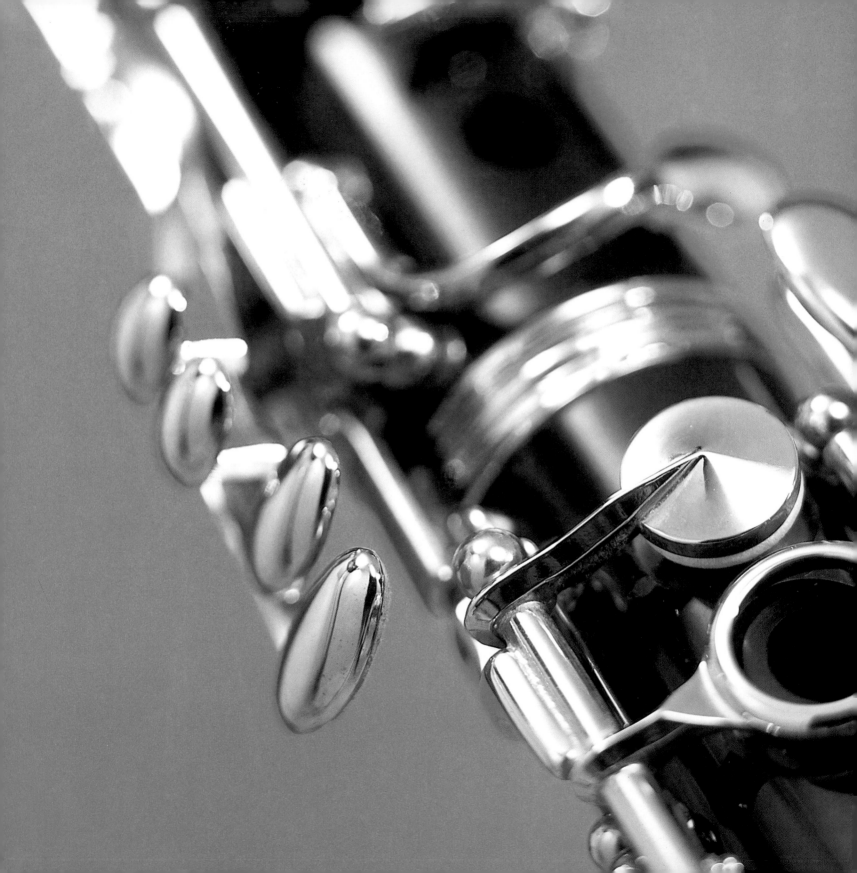

Overture

Playing and listening to music, as well as learning about it, is one of the most popular and exciting pastimes in the world today.

The clarinet is one of the most played of all woodwind instruments, and it can be heard in almost every kind of music—orchestral, wind band, chamber music, jazz, and pop. The instrument's musical reputation is well deserved. It has a clear and expressive sound that is ideal for solo work, whether playing in an orchestra or a small ensemble. The clarinet is particularly suitable for children to learn—unlike many other instruments, "real tunes" can be learned in a very short time.

We are not sure exactly who made the first clarinet, but it was probably a German instrument maker, Johann Christoph Denner, living in Nuremberg in about 1700. The clarinet was developed from an older folk instrument, the chalumeau. A great variety of folk clarinets are still played today in various parts of the world. In India the pungi is made from two parallel canes glued together, while a large gourd surrounds and protects the reeds. This is the traditional snake charmer's pipe.

The clarinet was at one time made from boxwood or rosewood, but today it is made from a heavy wood called African blackwood. A good-quality plastic clarinet is also available, although it may be some years before it is taken up by professional players. On pages 18 and 19 you will see photographs of a modern clarinet maker's workshop. Some of the tools you see in the pictures have not changed in design for over two hundred years.

The audio compact disc from EMI that accompanies this book features extracts of music written by ten great composers. The short section "ON THE CD," which appears in the text for each composer, tells you a little about the music.

Whether you are already a clarinetist, just beginning lessons, or simply interested in clarinet music, *The Living Clarinet* will add to the range of your knowledge and understanding of this remarkable instrument.

The Clarinet Family

Sopranino
The sopranino clarinet is a popular member of the military band, where its high, shrill tone adds sharpness to the mellow sound of the other woodwind and brass instruments. It is seldom used in orchestras, although composers occasionally call for its bright and breezy sound, often giving it a descriptive role to play.

Above: The word "sopranino" means "a little soprano"—that is, a very high instrument. The sopranino clarinet is the highest clarinet in general use today. It measures about nineteen inches long, three-quarters of the length of the orchestral clarinet.

Above: The clarinet's full name is "soprano clarinet." The name "clarinet" derives from the Italian word clarinetto, which means "little trumpet." The name was chosen to describe the clarinet's powerful but gentle sound. The instrument measures about twenty-six inches long.

Clarinet
The clarinet's reedy sound is produced by a thin piece of cane that vibrates to the force of the player's breath. Clarinetists have a selection of reeds of various strengths to choose from, depending on whether they want the sound of their instrument to be strident or more gentle. The clarinet blends well with almost all other instruments, especially flute, bassoon, horn, and strings.

Alto Clarinet
The alto clarinet was invented in 1810 by the German clarinetist and instrument maker Iwan Müller. It is lower in pitch and longer and larger than the soprano clarinet. To allow the instrument to be held easily, the mouthpiece is situated in an extra piece of tubing called a "crook," which is bent back toward the player. To avoid directing the sound of the instrument toward the floor, the flared "bell" is curved up and points in the direction of the listener.

Basset Horn

The basset horn is perfectly described by its name— "basset" means "little bass" (referring to its deep notes). Today, the basset horn looks similar to the alto clarinet, although a little larger. The basset horn was a favorite instrument of Mozart, who included it in his *Requiem*. Mendelssohn also wrote for the basset horn, and Richard Strauss used it in several of his operas. Today, basset horn parts are sometimes played by the alto clarinet.

Left: The basset horn's original curved construction was replaced in the early nineteenth century by a straight design that has remained the usual shape of the instrument ever since.

Bass Clarinet

The bass clarinet, larger than the alto clarinet and basset horn, is the lowest member of the clarinet family in general use. The earliest bass clarinets date from the end of the eighteenth century and were probably intended as wind band instruments. During the course of the nineteenth century, however, the bass clarinet slowly began to appear in orchestral scores. The French composer Giacomo Meyerbeer led the way in 1836 by writing an important part for it in his opera *Les Huguenots*.

Left: Because the bass clarinet is of considerable weight, it is held either in a sling around the player's neck or supported by a metal spike.

Contrabass Clarinet

The contrabass clarinet, the most recently invented instrument of the clarinet family, dates from the late nineteenth century. It is a curiously shaped instrument, looking nothing at all like a clarinet. "Contra" means "lower octave": to produce such low notes, the tube of the clarinet needs to be very long.

Left: Early versions of the contrabass clarinet looked like a larger version of the bass clarinet. Recent instruments are made entirely of metal, with the tube curled around itself and the bell at the top.

Wind Instruments Around the World

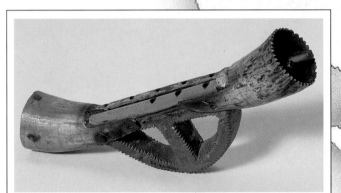

Pibcorn *(Wales)*
The Welsh pibcorn has a horn at both ends. The name is made up of "pib," meaning "pipe," and "corn," an old word for "horn." The reed is hidden inside the horn at the blowing end of the instrument. Players do not take the reed between their lips, but blow the instrument by pressing it tightly against their mouth.

Alboka *(Spain)*
The alboka, from northern Spain, originated in the Middle East. Like the Welsh pibcorn, it belongs to the hornpipe family and has long been associated with shepherds. Played with the blowing horn pressed tightly against the mouth, it has a distinct nasal sound.

Zummara *(Egypt)*
The Egyptian zummara is a double clarinet, made up of two pipes that are sounded simultaneously. Players use "circular breathing" to play the instrument—breathing in through their nose and out through their mouth at the same time. This clever technique means an uninterrupted flow of sound can be produced.

Diple *(Dalmatia)*
As a clarinet, the Dalmatian diple varies considerably in design from region to region; it can also take the form of a bagpipe. Its reedy, strident tone makes it well suited to outdoor playing. For this reason it is often used by shepherds for signaling and at village celebrations.

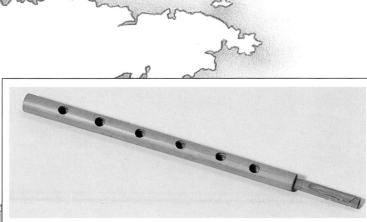

Xiao *(China)*
Xiao (pronounced "hiss-ow") means "little flute." This is one of China's most ancient wind instruments, dating back 3,000 years. It was at one time played by shepherds, but now it is more likely to be bought as a toy. The xiao in the picture is a child's instrument that was bought in Shanghai in 1902.

Pungi *(India)*
The Indian pungi is made of two parallel canes glued together. A large dried gourd surrounds the reeds, the player blowing into the neck of the gourd. The left pipe of the instrument plays a drone only (one note sounding all the time throughout the piece), while the right pipe plays the melody. The pungi is the traditional snake charmer's pipe.

Instrumental Groups

Duets

A duet is a piece for two performers. In the picture below, the clarinet plays a duet with the bagpipes. Duets were popular in the eighteenth century, but in the last two centuries duet writing seems to have been neglected.

Clarinet and Piano

Woodwind instruments like the clarinet blend well with the piano, and composers have written a variety of imaginative works for this combination of instruments, often writing for specific performers. Sonatas tend to be the most serious works; other music is in a much lighter vein, such as the Rhapsody for clarinet and piano by Claude Debussy.

Music for Solo Clarinet

Composers seldom write for solo unaccompanied "melody" instruments (instruments that can only play one line of music at a time, like the clarinet). This is probably because two players are easier to listen to than one, but also because an accompaniment allows a soloist to take an occasional rest. Writing for an unaccompanied solo instrument is very difficult, but some twentieth-century composers such as Igor Stravinsky have written successfully for solo clarinet.

Trios

A trio is a piece for three instruments, although "clarinet trio" does not usually mean a piece for three clarinets, but rather a trio in which a single clarinet is given a prominent part. Mozart wrote the first clarinet trio, still heard in concerts today, for clarinet, piano, and viola.

Quartets and Quintets

Although early composers for the clarinet, such as Carl Stamitz, wrote quartets and quintets for the instrument, these works are seldom heard today. It is Mozart again, with his Quintet for piano, oboe, clarinet, horn, and bassoon, who alone represents early clarinet chamber music. Quintets were later composed by Beethoven and Brahms and a few twentieth-century composers. In 1941 the French composer Olivier Messiaen wrote his *Quartet for the End of Time* for clarinet, violin, cello, and piano while in a prisoner-of-war camp.

The Clarinet in Jazz

The clarinet was for many years a leading instrument in jazz, popularized by such solo performers as Sidney Bechet, Benny Goodman, and Woody Herman. Jazz musicians were impressed with the smooth sounds readily available from the instrument, its wide dynamic range and robust tone. Today the clarinet is no longer a leading member of the jazz scene, although it remains an essential member of the Dixieland band.

Clarinet Concertos

The word "concerto" was originally used to describe a performance "together." Over the last 250 years, however, it has come to mean a composition usually for one solo instrument and orchestra. Clarinet concertos have been written throughout this period, although the only eighteenth-century concerto regularly heard today is by Mozart. In the twentieth century there have been several exciting new concertos for clarinet, including Stravinsky's *Ebony* Concerto, a jazz-style work written for clarinetist Benny Goodman.

The History of the Clarinet

Nuremberg in 1725, where the first clarinet was made.

Johann Christoph Denner

Music historians believe that the first clarinet was made in 1700 by Johann Christoph Denner, a German instrument maker living in Nuremberg. The first mention of the clarinet is in an order dated 1710 for twenty-three woodwind instruments, including clarinets, made by Jacob Denner, Johann's son. The clarinet was modeled on an earlier instrument called the chalumeau.

The Chalumeau

The chalumeau was at its best playing low notes, whereas the high notes were of poor quality. Johann Denner discovered that by adding an additional finger hole in the upper end of the tube, a higher range of notes could be reached. To improve the reliability of the high notes, the thick, crudely shaped reed of the chalumeau was made narrower and more slender. The first clarinet was in fact simply a high-sounding chalumeau.

Early clarinets were shriller and more penetrating than the instruments we

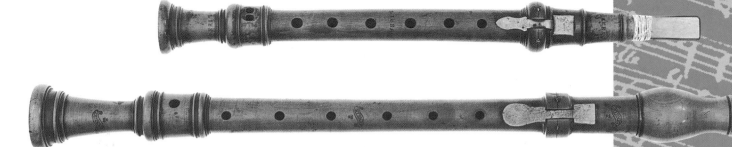

know today. They sounded more like a trumpet when heard from a distance.

Johann Denner died in 1707, but his work was carried on by his son, who reshaped the end of the tube into a bell (which looked like a small trumpet bell) to improve the projection of sound, and increased the range of notes.

To improve the accuracy of drilling the tube, and to make tuning easier, the body of the new instrument was made in several closely fitting jointed sections. The pitch of the instrument is related to the overall length of the tube and the makers came up with the ingenious idea of duplicating one of the clarinet joints in a variety of lengths – these were known by their French name, *corps de rechange.*

Above: The chalumeau, predecessor of the clarinet, showing the characteristically wide reed. The instrument sounds like a low clarinet.

Below: High-pitched clarinets:
a) sopranino
b) soprano in B flat
c) soprano in A

a)

b)

c)

A clarinet player from The Clarinet Instructor, *published in 1780.*

The English clarinetist T. L. Willman, in an illustration from his clarinet-playing book (c.1825).

During the eighteenth century, instrument makers continued to remodel and improve the clarinet, concentrating particularly on the fingering system. By 1750 the clarinet had made great strides since Denner's first model, and composers were beginning to include it in their works. The clarinet was more acceptable as an orchestral instrument now that it could tune to any orchestral pitch. Orchestras in Paris and the famed Mannheim orchestra already employed regular clarinetists. Military bands were also interested in the clarinet, with its relatively easy playing technique, increasingly using it in preference to the oboe. In 1764 the first clarinet-playing book, by the German virtuoso Valentin Roeser, was published.

By the end of the eighteenth century, to accommodate the demand for precision tuning, clarinet makers built clarinets in different keys. Because of the construction of the clarinet and its fingering system, it was easy playing in some keys and more difficult in others.

Iwan Müller

In 1809 the young German clarinetist Iwan Müller produced a clarinet with a new mechanical action and finger holes placed more accurately than ever before. The result was an instrument of improved intonation (tuning), which understandably became very popular. In 1822 Müller published a book on clarinet playing that featured the new instrument; he was granted permission to dedicate the book to King George IV. Müller's clarinet remained popular until the beginning of the twentieth century.

Theobald Boehm

In 1832 the instrument maker Theobald Boehm was working on improving the flute mechanism. When his work was complete, the French clarinetist Hyacinthe Klosé and the Paris instrument maker Louis-Auguste Buffet adapted the Boehm flute mechanism to the clarinet. The idea was successful, although players were generally reluctant at first to take up an instrument that would mean learning an entirely new fingering system.

As the nineteenth century wore on, other instrument makers, including Adolphe Sax, continued to adjust and modify the clarinet. Today, a variety of different instruments and fingering systems are in use, although the Boehm system remains the most popular.

a)   *b)*   *c)*   *d)*

Above: George IV of England by Thomas Gainsborough, 1781.

Left: Low-pitched clarinets:
a) alto
b) basset horn
c) bass
d) contrabass

How the Clarinet Works

Wind instruments produce their sound from a vibrating column of air inside a hollow body. In the case of the clarinet the air is set in motion by a reed, activated by the player's breath. The instrument modifies and amplifies the vibrations from the reed, turning them into sound.

The length of a tube (the body of the instrument) controls the pitch—how high or low the note is. A long tube will produce low notes, and a short tube high notes. By opening the finger holes in preset patterns, a scale of notes can be played. By pressing the "speaker key," the clarinetist is able to play notes higher up the instrument.

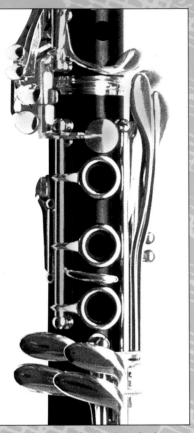

The **keywork** on the clarinet looks complicated, but in fact is designed to make the clarinet easier to play. Many keys cover holes that the fingers cannot reach.

The shape of the **bell** helps to project the sound outward from the instrument.

Fingers press the **keys** to open and close the holes. Some keys are coupled to others and are activated automatically when another key is pressed. The clarinet has seventeen keys.

Lower (or **right-hand**) **joint**

The modern clarinet is made in five sections, or **joints**. The **"tenon-and-socket" joints** fit together tightly to make sure there is no leakage of air, which would affect the tone of the instrument.

The top teeth rest on the top of the wedge-shaped **mouthpiece**. The reed (which is underneath) rests on the lower lip, which is slightly curved over the teeth.

The **barrel** is used for fine-tuning the instrument when necessary. By pulling the barrel out slightly, away from the top joint, the tube of the clarinet is made longer, and therefore the instrument will sound slightly lower. Some players use two barrels of different lengths to maintain tuning.

The **ligature** holds the reed tightly in place.

Upper (or **left-hand**) **joint**

The **reed** fits over a slot in the mouthpiece, which forms the end of the tube. The edges of the reed are secured by the ligature, but the main area of the reed is left free to vibrate.

Sound Wave of a Clarinet Note

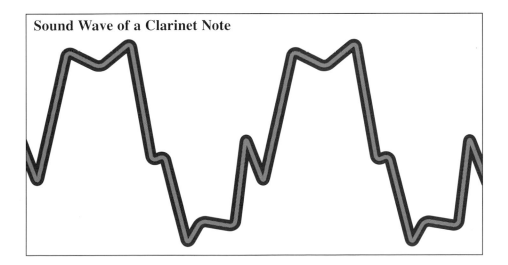

The **mouthpiece cap** protects the reed when the instrument is being carried or is not in use.

How the Clarinet Is Made

The **barrel** serves little or no real acoustic purpose but remains as a decorative feature and an occasional tuning device. The wood is first crudely shaped and drilled, then worked and bored to its final shape and decorated.

The elegant **bell** begins life as a pyramid-shaped block of wood. To achieve the exact trumpet shape requires considerable woodworking proficiency.

Right: The tube of the **upper joint** is first shaped to leave three wide bands of wood running close together at one end. Each band is then carefully pared to leave three raised **finger rests**, which ensure that the finger holes, when covered, remain airtight.

The clarinet was at one time made from boxwood or rosewood, but today the modern clarinet is made from the heavy African blackwood. For almost fifty years instrument makers have experimented with suitable plastics to find a replacement for wood that sounds just as good. Today, a good-quality plastic clarinet is available, although it may be some years before it is taken up by professional players.

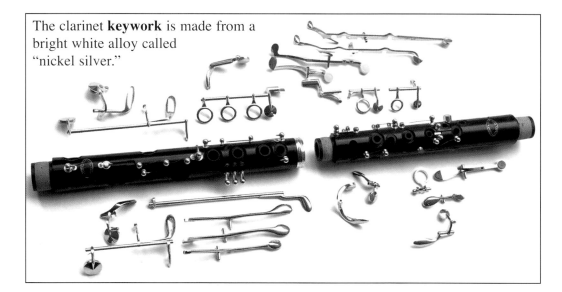

The clarinet **keywork** is made from a bright white alloy called "nickel silver."

Below: The **tenon-and-socket joints** use a band of cork to help maintain airtightness and a close fit. Here, the cork for one of the joints is being smoothed and trimmed on the lathe.

Fine adjustments are made to one of the **keys.** The keywork of the clarinet must be reliable and responsive to a player's touch.

The workshop displays a wealth of tools.

The clarinet maker uses a **reamer** to enlarge one of the holes, to modify the pitch.

The pads are tested with a very thin piece of paper to ensure they are pressing correctly on the holes.

19

How the Clarinet Is Played

The clarinet is one of the most popular of all woodwind instruments, and it can be heard in almost every kind of music, whether orchestral, wind band, chamber music, jazz, or pop. It has a clear and expressive sound that is ideal for solo work. The lowest notes, which have a reedy hollow sound, are unlike those of any other instrument. The clarinet is particularly suitable for young children to learn, for unlike many other instruments, "real" tunes can be played in a very short time.

Breathing
Clarinetists breathe through the mouth when they play. How a clarinetist breathes is one of the most important parts of playing the instrument, because it affects every detail of performance. Both the taking in of breath and its controlled release are equally important.

Tonguing
Clarinet players "tongue" a note by first placing the tip of their tongue lightly against the reed, and then pulling it back to release the breath and so sound the note. Tonguing is used to make sure that notes begin with precision and crispness.

Phrasing
Phrasing is common to nearly all instruments. A phrase is like a musical sentence; it gives music shape and expression. Clarinet players phrase notes by joining them together smoothly in one breath.

Louds and Softs
The clarinet has the greatest powers of *crescendo* (getting louder) and *diminuendo* (getting softer) of all the woodwind instruments. The clarinet is also much admired for its *pianissimo* (very soft) playing.

Staccato

The Italian word *staccato* means "detached." In clarinet playing, staccato notes are all tongued separately. The use of a certain amount of staccato adds elegance to clarinet playing.

Tremolo

This Italian word means "trembling." To clarinet players tremolo means playing two alternate notes in rapid succession. Played low down, a tremolo can sound mysterious and almost sinister, while played high up, it is shrill and exciting.

Vibrato

Vibrato, another Italian word, means "shaking." If you listen carefully to a clarinetist using vibrato, you will hear a slight wavering (rising and falling) of pitch.

Fingering

The right thumb fits snugly under the thumb hook on the underside of the lower joint and carries the weight of the clarinet.

Arpeggios, Leaps, and Scales

The clarinet is a very agile instrument. Leaping from one note to another, even with large gaps in between, is no problem for this accommodating instrument. Composers have occasionally used clarinet leaps for comic effects. Playing scales and arpeggios is also easy on the clarinet.

Glissando

"Glissando" is actually the French word *glisser,* meaning "to slide," deliberately made to sound Italian! A glissando is a slide (like a fast scale) over several notes. One of the most famous glissandos ever written is for clarinet—the beginning of George Gershwin's *Rhapsody in Blue.*

Multiphonics

It is possible with care to play more than one note at a time on the clarinet (and on other wind instruments also). Such "chords" of notes are called *multiphonics* ("multiple sounds"), and they produce a strange and almost eerie sound. To play them requires complex fingering.

Mozart
1756–1791

Mozart met the Austrian clarinetist Anton Stadler and became good friends with him (like Mozart, he was a Freemason). Mozart also wrote important clarinet parts in his operas for Stadler, as well as several chamber works and, of course, the much-loved Clarinet Concerto.

Right: *Frontispiece from Mozart's opera* La clemenza di Tito (The Clemency of Tito), *which includes a virtuoso clarinet part written especially for Anton Stadler.*

Wolfgang Amadeus Mozart showed his musical gifts at a very early age, when he began taking formal keyboard and theory lessons with his father, Leopold; by the age of four, we are told, he could play his lessons perfectly. When he composed his first pieces, he was unable to write the music down, so his father wrote it down for him.

While Mozart was copying out a symphony by the German composer Carl Friedrich Abel, he first encountered the clarinet. At the time, in 1764, the Mozarts were living in London, and it is possible that Mozart first heard the clarinet at a London concert.

Mozart wrote his first work for the clarinet in 1771, a Divertimento (a light piece written for entertainment purposes). Six years later he visited Mannheim, Germany, and was impressed by the clarinet playing in the famous orchestra at the electoral palace. To his father he wrote, "Alas, if only we also had clarinets."

The first work Mozart wrote for Anton Stadler was a Trio, scored for the unusual combination of clarinet, viola, and piano. Mozart wrote this beautiful work in 1786 at a time when he was virtually penniless. The Trio is occasionally known by its strange name of Kegelstatt

(Skittle Alley) Trio, because it is said the work was composed at a skittles match (an English game similar to bowling).

Mozart only gradually began to use clarinets in his orchestral works, including them in just four of his symphonies. His last work for clarinet—the Clarinet Concerto—is his most famous, and one of the best-known works ever written for the instrument.

ON THE CD
Track 1
Clarinet Quintet in A
I. Allegro

Mozart wrote the Clarinet Quintet, for clarinet and strings, in 1789, and Anton Stadler gave the work its first performance in Vienna the same year. In the opening of the first movement the clarinet plays a beautiful decorative accompaniment figure; it assumes more important thematic material later in the movement.

Beethoven was the first major composer to score for the clarinet in all his mature orchestral compositions.

Christian Gottlob Neefe (1748–1798) said of Beethoven, "This young genius will surely become a second Amadeus Mozart if he continues as he has begun."

Beethoven
1770–1827

Ludwig van Beethoven received his first music lessons from his father. At eleven he began studies with the court organist of Bonn, Germany, Christian Gottlob Neefe, who arranged for the boy to have one of his earliest compositions published.

Beethoven was born into the age of the clarinet. For almost a hundred years the clarinet had hovered on the sidelines of music. But with Beethoven's support its acceptance into the orchestra was finally assured. His Wind Octet (a piece for eight instruments), written for oboes, clarinets, bassoons, and horns, was composed when the composer was only twenty-two. In the same year, Beethoven wrote three duos (duets) for clarinet and bassoon.

Most of Beethoven's compositions for wind were written on commission, and commissions (paid requests for compositions) made up a valuable source of a composer's income.

Throughout his life Beethoven moved easily among the nobility and the rich. The Wind Quintet written in 1796, for instance, is dedicated to Prince von Schwarzenberg. A dedication by Beethoven almost always indicated a

Right: *A room in the house where Beethoven was born. The building is now a Beethoven museum.*

Bonn, where Beethoven was born in 1770. His father, Johann, was determined that young Ludwig should become a child prodigy like Mozart.

paid commission.

After the turn of the century Beethoven wrote virtually no more wind music. This may have been because the popular serenades and divertimentos of Haydn and Mozart's day were no longer in fashion. Another explanation may be, as Beethoven said in a letter to his publishers, that he had simply "moved on" to bigger and better things. Of course, Beethoven did not abandon the clarinet completely—it still had an extremely important role to play in his orchestral music.

Beethoven performed in public concert halls such as the Theater an der Wien (above) as well as in the houses of the Viennese nobility, often playing his own compositions.

Right: *Beethoven's house in Bonn. The composer was born in the attic on the right of the picture.*

ON THE CD
Track 2
Clarinet Trio in B flat
I. Allegro con brio

Beethoven wrote his Trio for clarinet, piano, and cello in 1797, on a commission from the Countess von Thun. In the score Beethoven indicates that the clarinet part can also be played by the violin.

Crusell was born in Finland to a family of bookbinders and became one of Finland's most highly regarded composers. He first heard the clarinet at the age of four and began formal clarinet lessons at the age of eight. Within a short time he had impressed his teacher and family with his astounding progress.

Crusell
1775–1838

Stockholm in Crusell's day. Crusell's informative autobiography tells us much about life in this thriving city.

Bernhard Henrik Crusell's music career began at the early age of twelve, when he joined a military band in the Finnish town of Sveaborg as a clarinetist. In 1791 he moved with the band to Stockholm, where he continued to concentrate on improving his playing technique. In 1793 he had his first major performing break, when he was appointed principal clarinetist in the Duke Regent's band in Stockholm.

By 1798 Crusell had moved to Berlin, where he began clarinet lessons with the noted teacher Franz Tausch. And in 1803 he studied with the French player Jean Xavier Lefèvre in Paris. Gradually Crusell was making a name for himself as a distinguished soloist, but his interest in composition was growing, too, and he took lessons with several eminent composers, including François-Joseph Gossec, a popular Parisian musical figure of the day.

Crusell's important works are the

Composers have often used folk tunes in their compositions. The song Crusell uses in his Variations for clarinet may well have been sung in scenes such as this.

Left: *Mikhail Ivanovich Glinka (1804–1857), one of the first major Russian composers, greatly admired Crusell's music. Speaking of one of Crusell's clarinet quartets, he said, "This music produced an unbelievable effect on me."*

Alexander I, Czar of Russia from 1801 to 1825.

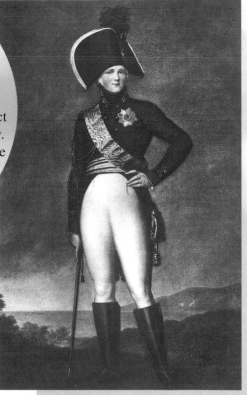

ON THE CD
Track 3
Clarinet Concerto No. 2
in F minor
III. Rondo: Allegretto

Through his association with the Swedish court Crusell came into contact with royalty and the nobility of his day. The Clarinet Concerto No. 2, one of the finest of Crusell's compositions for the instrument, is dedicated to Alexander I, Czar of Russia.

three clarinet concertos, written in 1811, 1816, and 1829. His Clarinet Concerto No. 1 is dedicated to a Swedish count, a close friend who often invited Crusell to his home, while the third concerto is dedicated to the Crown Prince of Sweden and Norway, whose band Crusell directed and conducted each summer.

Crusell also wrote a Triple Concerto (which he called a *sinfonia concertante*) for clarinet, horn, and bassoon. Another work, a set of Variations for clarinet and orchestra, uses a Swedish drinking song as its theme. As a composer, Crusell was admired particularly for his melodic invention.

Throughout his life Crusell held important playing and directing posts, including that of music director for the chapel of the Swedish court and for the royal regiment. Toward the end of his life he wrote an autobiography, which offers music historians many fascinating details about his life and times.

Spohr
1784–1859

As a composer, Spohr was highly regarded—he was made an honorary member of thirty-eight music societies in Germany and abroad.

The town of Brunswick, where Spohr was born. Although the family moved elsewhere in 1796, Spohr's parents sent him back to study here.

Louis Spohr was only ten years old when he made his first attempts at composition. Both his parents were musical, and they sent their son to Brunswick, Germany, to study music; here, at fifteen, after appearing in a successful concert of his own works, he was employed by the duke as one of his chamber musicians.

Although Spohr began his adult professional life as a violinist, his developing musicianship soon led him more in the direction of composition. He idolized Mozart, and it was perhaps Mozart's great Clarinet Concerto that inspired him to start composing himself: between 1810 and 1828 he wrote four works for the clarinet.

The highly respected German clarinetist Simon Hermstedt, to whom Spohr dedicated his first concerto, gave the premiere of all four concertos. The clarinet as a solo instrument was still relatively new in Spohr's day, although

La Scala, in Milan, Italy, still one of the greatest opera houses in the world, was the scene of one of the Spohrs' most successful concerts in 1816.

it was well established in the orchestra. Spohr was clearly fond of the new instrument, giving it an important solo part in one of his songs.

In 1806 Spohr married Dorette Scheidler, a harpist, and they made many successful tours together, while Spohr continued to compose prolifically. During this period he wrote two of his most respected chamber works for clarinet: the Nonet (for nine instruments) was written in 1813, and the Octet (for eight instruments) followed the next year. Spohr also used the clarinet in his Septet (seven instruments) of 1853 and Quintet of 1820.

Spohr also wrote several virtuoso solo works for clarinet. "Display" works for individual instruments were always popular on concert programs and much enjoyed by audiences. In Spohr's Clarinet Variations of 1809 he used a theme from his own opera *Alruna*. Despite his popularity during his lifetime, after his death almost all of Spohr's works fell into obscurity.

Dorette Scheidler, Spohr's wife, was a competent pianist and violinist as well as being a harpist. Spohr was only twenty when he married.

Below: *The music room in Spohr's house, with the composer's grand piano in the corner.*

ON THE CD
Track 4
Octet in E
Adagio—Allegro

Spohr wrote his Octet in 1814. The instruments the composer uses— mixed woodwind, brass, and strings— are unusual as a chamber group. The clarinet, two horns, violin, two violas, cello, and double bass, however, blend perfectly together.

Weber
1786–1826

Weber was related to Mozart by marriage, and like Mozart, he died young. Weber's chamber works include several compositions for clarinet, although he was really more interested in composing operas and large orchestral works than small chamber compositions.

Carl Maria von Weber's father was music director of his own traveling theatrical group, the Weber Theater Company. While touring southern Germany, young Carl took his first music lessons at the age of three with his stepbrother Fridolin, who said the boy would never become a musician! But by the age of eleven Weber was studying with Michael Haydn, younger brother of the great Joseph Haydn. By the time he was fifteen, he was determined that composition would be his life.

Over the next few years Weber took on a curious mixture of posts, including the conductorship of the opera at Breslau, Poland.

He was also secretary to the brother of the King of Württemberg. Somehow, through the foolishness of his father, he found himself being charged with embezzlement and expelled from the kingdom! Forced to seek residence elsewhere, Weber settled in Darmstadt, where he met the great German clarinetist Heinrich Joseph Baermann. Their friendship was to prove extremely fruitful.

In 1811 Weber and Baermann gave a successful joint concert in Munich that

Salzburg cathedral, where Weber was a chorister. In 1806 he accidentally drank a glass of nitric acid thinking it was wine. This destroyed the composer's singing voice as well as seriously affecting his speech.

***Above:** Ludwigstrasse in Munich at the time of Weber's meeting with the clarinetist Heinrich Baermann. Baermann was principal clarinetist of the Munich court orchestra.*

Above: Wolf's Glen scene from Weber's opera Der Freischütz. *In highly Romantic works, like this tale based on German folklore, Weber was at his best as a dramatic orchestrator.*

Below: King Maximilian I of Bavaria.

included Weber's new Clarinet Concertino (a small concerto), written specially for Baermann. King Maximilian I, present in the audience, immediately commissioned two full-scale clarinet concertos from Weber. After further traveling and performing, Weber returned to Munich to set off again with Baermann on a joint concert tour.

It is likely that Weber's friendship with Baermann prompted most of his compositions for clarinet, although Weber also met the clarinetist Simon Hermstedt and was invited to compose for him. Weber also wrote several small chamber works for the clarinet, including a set of Variations on a theme from his opera *Silvana* and a Clarinet Quintet.

ON THE CD
Track 5
Grand Duo Concertant
III. Rondo: Allegro

Weber wrote three works for clarinet and piano. The finest and most well-known is the *Grand Duo Concertant*. The *grand* tells us the composer considered this an important work, and *Duo* (duet) tells us that both clarinet and piano are of equal musical importance.

31

Rossini
1792–1868

It is likely that Rossini was first introduced to the clarinet through his father, who played the horn in a military band; in these bands the clarinet was well established.

At an early age Gioachino Rossini learned the French horn from his father, and by the time he was twelve, he was composing his first pieces.

When the family moved to Bologna, Italy, in 1804, Rossini entered the music school, where he studied other orchestral instruments and began to make his first efforts at orchestration. During this period he wrote several student works and won a prize for a cantata.

Left: Napoleon at the Bridge of Arcole, *by Baron Antoine-Jean Gros. The Napoleonic Wars caused tremendous political upheaval throughout Europe. The Rossini family was drawn into this turmoil, especially Rossini's father, who spent a short time in prison in 1800.*

Right: Scene from The Barber of Seville, *considered one of Rossini's greatest operas. At its first performance rival supporters of a similar opera based on the same play nearly caused a riot in the theater.*

In his orchestrations Rossini especially favored the clarinet and the woodwind family; we find many fine clarinet solos in his opera scores. One of Rossini's most famous clarinet tunes is in the overture to his comic opera *The Barber of Seville,* written in 1816.

But there are other, equally fine ones in *The Thieving Magpie* and in another popular opera, *La Cenerentola* (Cinderella).

Rossini composed several works specifically for the clarinet. In 1809, while still a student, he wrote a set of Variations for clarinet, string quartet, and orchestra—*Variazioni a più istrumenti obbligati*. Three years later he wrote a similar piece, *Andante e Tema con variazioni* (Andante and Theme with Variations), this time for four solo wind instruments—flute, clarinet, horn, and bassoon.

Rossini also composed several military band pieces, including three marches written in 1837, commissioned for the marriage of the Duc d'Orléans. And in the last year of his life he wrote a band piece entitled *La corona d'Italia* (The Crown of Italy), probably composed for an official function.

Right: Bologna in the nineteenth century. In 1804, the Rossini family moved to Bologna, where Gioachino began his first formal music studies.

Rossini's funeral in Paris was attended by thousands of mourners. In his will the composer left a large endowment for the establishment of a music school at his birthplace, Pesaro, Italy.

ON THE CD
Track 6
Introduction, Theme, and Variations for clarinet and orchestra

Rossini wrote this piece—another work in the popular variation style—in 1809, when he was a student at Bologna's Liceo Musicale.

Mendelssohn
1809–1847

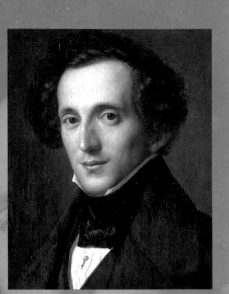

Mendelssohn did not write much for solo clarinet, but the instrument was very important to him in his orchestral music. Particularly loved among Mendelssohn's orchestral works is the Italian Symphony; *the clarinets and other wind instruments are heard in the lively accompaniment figure of the opening.*

Felix Mendelssohn was born into an artistic and well-to-do German banking family. This enabled him to have the finest musicians as teachers, who encouraged him to pursue his musical talents.

At fifteen Mendelssohn wrote his first piece for clarinet—a Sonata with piano accompaniment—for his friend, the fourteen-year-old Carl Baermann, son of Heinrich. The same year, while on holiday, Mendelssohn wrote for clarinet again—an Overture for wind band.

Left: *Carl Friedrich Zelter (1758–1832), teacher and composer and a leading figure in Berlin's musical life, taught Mendelssohn theory and composition.*

Above: *Berlin, Unter den Linden. In 1811 the Mendelssohn family moved to Berlin, where Felix spent his childhood.*

Left and below: *On a trip to Scotland in 1829 Mendelssohn visited the Hebrides, and in particular Fingal's Cave, the huge sea cavern on the Isle of Staffa. The cave and its surroundings made a great impression on Mendelssohn and inspired several musical thoughts, which he jotted down on the spot and later used in his* Hebrides *Overture.*

Mendelssohn composed several other overtures during his mature years. Some of this music includes descriptions of the sea; the smooth, flowing sound of the clarinet associates well with such images. In the exciting *Hebrides* Overture the clarinet introduces the beautiful second melody; and in the overture *The Fair Melusina*, written in 1833, the clarinet theme

Mendelssohn's house in Leipzig. The composer accepted the post of conductor of the famous Leipzig Gewandhaus orchestra in 1835.

represents the mermaid Melusina. The wind section of the orchestra also plays an important part in the overture *Calm Sea and Prosperous Voyage*.

In 1832 Mendelssohn wrote a Concert Piece for the unusual combination of clarinet, basset horn, and piano. This piece was nicknamed *The Battle of Prague*, as Mendelssohn had included in the score a theme by the Czech composer Frantisek Koczwara, who, forty-five years previously, had composed a sonata of the same name. The Concert Piece was written for Heinrich Baermann and his son Carl.

**ON THE CD
Track 7
*Concert Piece in D minor
for clarinet, basset horn, and
orchestra*
*Presto—Andante—Allegretto grazioso***

When Heinrich and Carl Baermann played through Mendelssohn's first Concert Piece, they were so taken with the music that they immediately commissioned a second, similar work. Mendelssohn wrote the Concert Piece in D minor in less than a month, presenting the score to his friends in January 1833.

Schumann
1810–1856

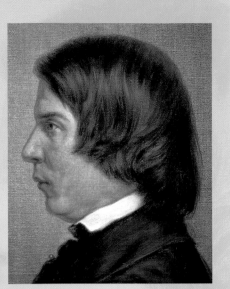

Schumann's output was prolific and included several chamber works for clarinet.

Below: *Zwickau, Saxony, where Schumann was born, the son of a bookseller. By the time he was eleven, Schumann had written his first orchestral works.*

Robert Schumann showed his musical talents at an early age (about six), but his parents were determined that he should become a lawyer. However, he gave up his law studies to follow a musical career. Schumann wanted passionately to become a piano virtuoso, but a tragedy destroyed all hopes of a concert career. A sling-like device of his own invention, designed to strengthen the fourth finger of his right hand, resulted in a permanent disability. Fortunately, he had a second musical interest, composition—and it was to this he now turned.

Above: *Friedrich Wieck (1785–1873), Schumann's piano teacher and Clara Schumann's father. It was while studying with Wieck that Schumann damaged his hand.*

Right: *Schumann with his wife, Clara, who gave him much encouragement as a composer, and who was herself a fine pianist.*

36

Left: Spring, *by Claude Monet. Schumann called his first symphony the* Spring *because he watched the countryside transform from winter into spring outside his room as he composed the music. The clarinet plays an important role throughout the work.*

Below: The Dresden Revolution, *1849, by Julius Scholtz. The year of writing the* Phantasiestücke *for clarinet was no easy year for Schumann and his wife, Clara. Returning from the country one day, they found Dresden in uproar, and only just escaped in time to avoid becoming involved in the violence themselves.*

By Schumann's day the clarinet was a fully established member of the orchestra. The clarinet has the same smooth sound as the flute and blends well with the other woodwind instruments. Composers were also beginning to appreciate the clarinet for its own beautiful sound, particularly appropriate in slow, lyrical melodies.

In 1849, during a prolific spell of composing, Schumann wrote three pieces for clarinet and piano that he called *Phantasiestücke* (Fantasy Pieces). In another chamber work written the same year—the three Romances for oboe and piano—Schumann suggested the optional instruments of clarinet and violin.

Schumann was very much a romantic, in tune with his times, and this is reflected in his fanciful titles. In 1853, in the closing years of his composing

life, he wrote the *Märchenerzählungen* (Fairy-tale Pieces), four pieces for piano, clarinet, and viola, with the option of violin for the clarinet part. They comprise Schumann's last chamber music work.

ON THE CD
Track 8
Phantasiestücke
III. Rasch und mit Feuer—
Coda: Schneller

The *Fantasy Pieces* for clarinet were always popular with Clara Schumann, who used to play them with the famous clarinetist Richard Mühlfeld. The third piece in *Phantasiestücke* is sprightly and quick, and Schumann marks it "with fire."

Brahms
1833–1897

Unfortunately for clarinet players and lovers of the instrument, Brahms only "discovered" the clarinet toward the end of his life. But he left several pieces of fine chamber music as a worthy addition to the clarinetist's repertoire.

Johannes Brahms's father was a double bass player in Hamburg, Germany, and it was from him that Johannes received his first musical instruction. At the age of fourteen the young composer played in a public concert—his own set of Piano Variations, based on a folk song.

The clarinet first appears in Brahms's early orchestral works, most prominently in the two Serenades for small orchestra, written when the composer was in his middle twenties. The Serenades remind us of Mozart, as Brahms also preferred to write in Classical forms. In the second Serenade the clarinets play a leading role right from the start; particularly beautiful is the clarinet and flute melody in the slow third movement.

Left: *Freiburg, one of the towns where Brahms and Richard Mühlfeld performed the clarinet sonatas on their tour of southern Germany in 1895.*

Right: *Chamber music playing was a popular pastime in the houses of the well-to-do. In this picture the cello player has fallen asleep at the end of an evening's entertainment.*

Meiningen, where, through his good friend the Duke of Meiningen, Brahms met the clarinetist Richard Mühlfeld, for whom he wrote his clarinet pieces.

The Trio in A minor is the first of Brahms's chamber works to include clarinet. Brahms wrote all his clarinet works for the same performer, the German virtuoso Richard Mühlfeld, whom he met at Meiningen. He was impressed not only by Mühlfeld's playing but also by the capabilities of the instrument itself. This trio, for clarinet, cello, and piano, was written in the summer of 1891 in Brahms's favorite holiday resort of Bad Ischl.

When the work was finished, Brahms was so pleased with his efforts that he began a second piece—a Quintet for clarinet and string quartet. In this work Brahms fully explores the expressive potential of the clarinet. At the opening of the first movement the instrument rises high above the violins —only to fall, later, to the rich, deep tones of its lowest register.

Brahms wrote all his solo clarinet pieces toward the end of his life, and perhaps for this reason these beautiful works have their own special poignancy.

Below: *This contemporary cartoon shows the composer on his way to The Red Hedgehog, a favorite inn. Brahms worked hard, but he also enjoyed a lively social life.*

ON THE CD
Track 9
Clarinet Quintet in B minor
III. Andantino—Presto non assai, ma con sentimento

The Clarinet Quintet, written in 1891, is often considered the most beautiful of all of Brahms's chamber works. The piece is written for clarinet, two violins, viola, and cello.

When Reger was a young man, Bach, Beethoven, and Brahms were the composers he respected most, and his aim was to incorporate their style into his own works. His clarinet works especially show the influence of Brahms.

Below: J. S. Bach, one of Reger's earliest influences. Reger admired Bach's use of counterpoint (the setting of several strands of music one against the other) and used the technique in his own works.

Reger
1873–1916

Max Reger's father, Joseph, was a keen amateur musician and played the oboe, clarinet, and double bass. The Regers were determined that their son should take music lessons at the earliest opportunity, although it was not until he was approaching his teens that Max began formal music training. As a student under the local organist, he composed his first music, but he also followed in his father's footsteps by training to be a teacher.

Reger had been introduced to the mellow sound of the clarinet through the playing of his father and music making at home. He held Brahms in great respect as one of Germany's foremost composers, and in 1895 he sent one of his compositions to Brahms. The composer replied with encouraging remarks and a signed photograph!

In 1888, as a boy of fifteen, Reger traveled to hear Richard Wagner's opera Parsifal at Bayreuth, Germany. It was after seeing the opera that Reger decided to become a musician.

Left: Reger had a quiet country upbringing in Bavaria in a household where music was always played and encouraged.

Within five years, and after Brahms's death, Reger wrote his own clarinet sonatas. They were performed two years later with Reger playing the piano and his friend Karl Wagner playing the clarinet.

In 1909, when Reger was director of music and composition at Leipzig University, he wrote a third clarinet sonata. The influence of Brahms in this work is clear before a note is heard—Brahms's sonatas and Clarinet Trio have alternative string parts and Reger wrote "clarinet or viola" on the score. Reger composed his final piece for clarinet in 1916, a Quintet. He died suddenly a few months later after paying a visit to friends.

Right: In 1896 Reger was conscripted into military service, which had a disruptive effect on his studies. As a student teacher he was required to do a year's training, but he was released after only nine months because of ill health.

**ON THE CD
Track 10
Clarinet Quintet in A
II. Vivace—un poco meno mosso
—Tempo primo: Vivace**

Reger's Quintet for clarinet, two violins, viola, and cello is a calm and serene piece, reminiscent of Brahms. Interestingly, the clarinet is not treated as the most important instrument here—the musical material is shared equally between each performer.

Great Players

JOSEPH BEER
1744–1812

Joseph Beer was the first important solo clarinetist. He was born in Bohemia (in the present-day Czech Republic), where he first learned the trumpet and later the clarinet. He moved to Paris, where he concentrated on improving his clarinet playing and became friends with Carl Stamitz, a keen composer of clarinet music. Beer soon made a name for himself as a virtuoso clarinetist, traveling all over Europe. From 1782 to 1792 he was clarinetist to Catherine the Great of Russia, and he was later employed by Frederick the Great of Prussia.

ANTON STADLER
1753–1812

Anton Stadler was born in Austria, where he and his brother Johann both studied the clarinet, frequently performing together. In 1773 they were employed by the Russian ambassador in Vienna, and having made a name for themselves as musicians of excellence, they were invited to join the orchestra of the royal court in 1787 as its first regular clarinetists.

Stadler designed a new instrument that could play much lower notes than the normal clarinet; he called his new model the "basset" clarinet. He also wrote for the regular clarinet.

SIMON HERMSTEDT
1778–1846

As a child, Simon Hermstedt learned several instruments, but it was as a clarinetist that he excelled. In 1801 notice of his playing reached a local member of the nobility, the Duke of Sondershausen, who engaged him as a court musician. The duke, impressed with his new musician, commissioned a concerto from the composer Spohr to be performed by Hermstedt and the ducal orchestra. As a performer, Hermstedt played throughout Germany, astounding audiences with his technical brilliance.

Great Players

THOMAS LINDSAY WILLMAN 1784–1840

Thomas Lindsay Willman was born into a musical family. His father was a German bandsman who settled in England in the middle of the eighteenth century, and his sister married the celebrated flutist Charles Nicholson.

At the age of twenty-one Willman played in the Dublin Theatre orchestra, and in 1916 he took a permanent appointment as bandmaster to the Coldstream Guards. The following year he became first clarinet in the orchestra of London's Royal Philharmonic Society and held this appointment until his death. In 1838 he gave the first English performance of Mozart's Clarinet Concerto.

HEINRICH BAERMANN 1784–1847

Like his close contemporary Simon Hermstedt, Heinrich Baermann was educated at a school for children of the military. By the age of fourteen he was an oboist in the band of the Prussian Life Guards, but he gave up the position to study the clarinet with the famous virtuoso Joseph Beer.

Baermann toured far and wide, performing works written for him by Weber, Mendelssohn, and Meyerbeer. In 1819 he visited England, where he played before the Prince Regent at Brighton and gave a series of concerts in London, playing several of his own works.

HYACINTHE ELÉONORE KLOSÉ 1808–1880

Hyacinthe Eléonore Klosé was born in Corfu. He moved to Paris as a young man and enlisted in a regimental band as a clarinetist. In 1831 he entered the Paris Conservatoire, where he was taught by Frédérick Berr. He played in orchestras and made a name for himself as a soloist. Later he succeeded his teacher at the conservatoire, where he remained for thirty years.

Klosé spent many years adapting the fingering of the new Boehm flute to the clarinet, as well as composing and publishing music for the instrument and writing a book on clarinet playing that is still used today.

Great Players

RICHARD MÜHLFELD
1856–1907

Both violin and clarinet were important instruments to Richard Mühlfeld. His first major employment was as a court violinist in his hometown of Meiningen, Germany, and six years later, when he was twenty-three, he became principal clarinetist in the orchestra of the Duke of Meiningen.

It was the conductor of the court orchestra who pointed out the impressive playing of Mühlfeld to Brahms, and possibly he suggested that the composer might like to write for clarinet. The results brought both composer and performer success and pleasure.

MANUEL GOMEZ
1859–1922

Manuel Gomez was born in Seville, Spain, where a visiting bandmaster gave him clarinet lessons. In 1882 he gained admission to the Paris Conservatoire. After completing his studies, he was appointed first clarinet at the Paris Opéra. In 1890 Gomez moved to London, where he met and became firm friends with the conductor Henry Wood. In 1903 Gomez and a group of friends planned a new London orchestra—the London Symphony Orchestra—which gave its first performance in 1904. Although he gave solo recitals throughout his life, Gomez was primarily a skilled orchestral player.

FREDERICK THURSTON
1901–1953

Frederick Thurston won an open scholarship to London's Royal College of Music. His professional life began with the Royal Philharmonic Orchestra and the Covent Garden Opera Orchestra. Later he played with the BBC's own Symphony Orchestra and returned to the Royal College of Music to teach.

Thurston inspired several British composers to write works for him, including Arnold Bax (Clarinet Sonata) and Arthur Bliss (Clarinet Quintet).

Great Players

BENNY GOODMAN
1909–1986

The American Benny Goodman entered the world of clarinet playing through jazz. At the age of twelve he made his professional debut; when he was still in his teens, he joined a professional band as a soloist.

In 1934 Goodman took a step in another direction and made several classical recordings, including Mozart's Clarinet Quintet, a shift in career that turned out to be astonishingly successful. He commissioned pieces from Béla Bartók, Aaron Copland, and Paul Hindemith and recorded many of the greatest works in the clarinet repertoire.

JACK BRYMER
born 1915

The British clarinetist Jack Brymer was born in the north of England to a musical family and taught himself to play the clarinet. In 1947 he was appointed principal clarinetist of the Royal Philharmonic Orchestra, after which he held the same position with the BBC Symphony Orchestra and later with the London Symphony Orchestra.

Brymer has been a founding member of several wind ensembles. He taught at the Royal Academy of Music and at the Royal Military School of Music. He has made three recordings of Mozart's Clarinet Concerto.

GERVASE DE PEYER
born 1926

Gervase de Peyer was born in London, where he studied under Frederick Thurston at the Royal College of Music. In 1950 he formed and played in the Melos Ensemble. He also directed the London Symphony Wind Ensemble. In 1955 he was appointed first clarinet with the London Symphony Orchestra, a position he held until 1971. As a soloist, he has given important first performances of clarinet works by British composers, including Thea Musgrave's Clarinet Concerto. De Peyer also teaches at London's Royal Academy of Music.

CD Track Listings

Figures in […] identify the track numbers from the EMI recording. Track lengths are listed in minutes and seconds.

EMI is one of the world's leading classical music companies, with a rich heritage and reputation for producing great and often definitive recordings performed by the world's greatest artists. As a result of this long and accomplished recording history, EMI has an exceptional catalog of classical recordings, exceptional in both quality and quantity. It is from this catalog that EMI has selected the recordings detailed in the track listing below. Many of the recordings featured are available on CD and cassette from EMI.

Wolfgang Amadeus Mozart 1756–1791
Clarinet Quintet in A K581
[1]   I. Allegro   6.49
Gervase de Peyer (clarinet)
Members of the Melos Ensemble of London
Ⓟ1964/1989*

Ludwig van Beethoven 1770–1827
Clarinet Trio in B flat Op. 11
[2]   I. Allegro con brio   8.58
The Nash Ensemble of London
Ⓟ1990†

Bernhard Henrik Crusell 1775–1838
Clarinet Concerto No. 2 in F minor Op. 5
[3]   III. Rondo: Allegretto   6.07
Antony Pay (clarinet)
Orchestra of the Age of Enlightenment Ⓟ1993†

Louis Spohr 1784–1859
Octet in E Op. 32
[4]   Adagio—Allegro   6.37
Members of the Melos Ensemble of London
Ⓟ1958/1995* [MONO]

Carl Maria von Weber 1786–1826
Grand Duo Concertant Op. 48
[5]   III. Rondo: Allegro   5.49
Michael Collins (clarinet), Kathryn Stott (piano)
Ⓟ1992

Gioachino Rossini 1792–1868
[6]   **Introduction, Theme, and Variations for
        clarinet and orchestra**   12.56
Gervase de Peyer (clarinet)
New Philharmonia Orchestra conducted by
Rafael Frühbeck de Burgos Ⓟ1969/1986*

Felix Mendelssohn 1809–1847
**Concert Piece in D minor
for clarinet, basset horn, and orchestra No. 2** Op. 114
[7]   Presto—Andante—Allegretto grazioso   8.26
Sabine Meyer (clarinet), Wolfgang Meyer (basset horn)
Württemberg Chamber Orchestra Heilbronn
conducted by Jörg Faerber Ⓟ1985+

Robert Schumann 1810–1856
Phantasiestücke Op. 73
[8]   III. Rasch und mit Feuer—Coda: Schneller   4.08
Michael Collins (clarinet), Kathryn Stott (piano) Ⓟ1992

Johannes Brahms 1833–1897
Clarinet Quintet in B minor Op. 115
[9]   III. Andantino—Presto non assai, ma con sentimento 4.44
Gervase de Peyer (clarinet)
Members of the Melos Ensemble of London Ⓟ1965/1989*

Max Reger 1873–1916
Clarinet Quintet in A Op. 146
[10] II. Vivace—Un poco meno mosso—
        Tempo primo: Vivace   5.33
Gervase de Peyer (clarinet)
Members of the Melos Ensemble of London Ⓟ1965/1995*

70.50
[DDD/*ADD]

Acknowledgments

The publisher would like to thank the following for their permission to use illustrative material reproduced in this book:
a= above, b=below, c=center, r=right, l=left

AKG, London: 12, 15*r*, 22*a*, 23*a* & *b* (and music throughout in panels and Index), 24*bl*, 25*l* & *c*, 25*b*, 26*r*, 27*a*, *r* & *b*, 28*a* & *r*, 29*b*, 30*a*, *b* & *r*, 32*r*, 34*a*, *b* & *bl*, 36*bl*, 37*b*, 38*a* & *b*, 39*a*, 40*a* & *r*; **Bridgeman Art library:** 32*al* (Hermitage, Leningrad), 37*a* (Fitzwilliam Museum, Cambridge, © DACS, London 1996), 38*r* (Towneley Hall Art Gallery & Museum, Burnley), 41*ar* (Stadtische Museum, Erfurt); **Deutsche Staatsbibliothek, Berlin:** 42*c* & *l*, 43*r*; **E.T. Archive:** 3*b*, 24*a*, 36*a*; **Mary Evans Picture Library:** 24*br*, 29*a* & *b*, 33*a* & *b*, 36*c* &*r*, 41*br*; *The New Grove Dictionary of Music:* 13, 14, 15*l*, 43*c*; **Robbie Jack:** 10*c*; **Leblanc, Paris:** 6*a*, 7; **Lebrecht Collection:** 11*a* (Nigel Luckhurst), 22*b*, 23*r*, 24*al*, 26*l*, 28*bl*, 29*ar*, 35*a*, *b* & *c*, 39*b*, 41*a*, 44*r*, 45*r* (Nigel Luckhurst); **Performing Arts Library:** 6*b* (James McCormick), 10*l* (Colin Willoughby), 10*r* (Fritz Curzon), 11*b* (Clive Barda), 11*r* (Sefton Samuels); **Pitt Rivers Museum:** 8*l*, *a* & *b*, 9*a*, *r* & *b*; **Staatliches Heimat-und Schlossmuseum, Sondershausen:** 43*l*; **Weston, Pamela:** *Clarinet Virtuosi of the Past*, **Robert Hale, London, 1971:** 44*l*.

Front cover photograph by Michael Banks (and panel photographs used on pages 1–5, 12, 15, 47). Back cover: boxwood clarinet and bell of clarinet: Howarth of London for Classical Musical Instruments (T. W. Howarth & Co. Ltd.); portrait of Beethoven: E.T. Archive.

Photographs on pages 16–21 by Phil Rudge.
Map on pages 8–9 by Bill Gregory.
Endpapers: score from Beethoven's Concerto No. 5 (*Emperor*) reproduced with permission from Eulenberg Editions Ltd.

The publishers are also grateful to:
EMI Records UK for their cooperation and expertise in compiling the CD.
Howarth of London for Classical Musical Instruments (T. W. Howarth & Co. Ltd.) and Jon Steward for photographs taken at their workshop on pages 3, 16–19, and also the clarinet featured on the back cover.
Kamera Kids for the model used on pages 17, 20–21.
The Kensington Music Shop for the clarinet used on pages 17, 20–21.
Dr. Hélène La Rue of the Pitt Rivers Museum, Oxford, for her help in providing the photographs used on pages 8–9.

Index

Abel, Carl Friedrich 22
accompaniment 10
African blackwood 5, 18
alboka 8
Alexander 1, Czar of Russia 27
alto clarinet 6, 7, 15
Andante e Tema con variazioni 33
arpeggios 21

Bad Ischl, Germany 39
Baermann, Carl 34, 35
Baermann, Heinrich 30, 31, 34, 35, 43
bagpipes 9, 10
Barber of Seville, The 32
barrel 17, 18
Bartók, Béla 45
bass clarinet 7, 15
basset clarinet 42
basset horn 7, 15
bassoon 10, 24, 27, 33
Bax, Arnold 44
Beer, Joseph 42, 43
Beethoven, Ludwig van 10, 24–25, 40
bell 6, 13, 16, 18
Berlin, Germany 34
Berr, Frédérick 43
Bliss, Arthur 44
Boehm, Theobald 15, 43
Bologna, Italy 32, 33
Bonn, Germany 25
Brahms, Johannes 10, 38–39, 40, 44
breathing 21
Breslau opera 30
Brighton, England 43
Brunswick, Germany 28
Brymer, Jack 45
Buffet, Louis-Auguste 15

cane 6, 9
cello 25, 39, 41
Cenerentola, La 32
chalumeau 5, 12, 13
chamber music 10, 29, 30, 31, 36, 38
China 9
circular breathing 8
Clarinet Concertino 31
Clarinet Concerto 23
Clarinet Concerto No. 1 27
Clarinet Concerto No. 2 27
clarinet duet 10, 24, 31
clarinet-playing book 14
clarinet quartet 10
clarinet quintet 10, 31
Clarinet Quintet in A (Mozart) 23
Clarinet Quintet in A (Reger) 41
Clarinet Quintet in B minor 39
clarinet solo 10, 34, 39
clarinet sonata 41
clarinet trio 10
Clarinet Trio in B flat 25
Clemenza di Tito, La 22

Concert Piece in D minor for clarinet,
    basset horn, and orchestra 35
concerto 11
contrabass clarinet 7, 15
Copland, Aaron 45
cork 18
Corona d'Italia, La 33
corps de rechange 13
crescendo 20
crook 6
Crusell, Bernhard Henrik 26–27

Dalmatia 9
de Peyer, Gervase 45
Debussy, Claude 10
Denner, Jacob 12
Denner, Johann Christoph 5, 12, 13,
    14
diminuendo 20
diple 9
Dixieland 11
d'Orléans, Duc 33
double bass 38, 40
Dresden, Germany 37
drone 9

Ebony Concerto 11
Egypt 8

Fair Melusina, The 35
finger holes 7, 12, 14, 18, 21
finger rests 18
fingering system 14, 15
Finland 26
flute 33, 37, 38
Frederick the Great of Prussia 42
Freiburg, Germany 38
Freischütz, Der 31
French horn 32

George IV 14, 15
Gershwin, George 21
Glinka, Mikhail Ivanovich 27
glissando 21
Gomez, Manuel 44
Goodman, Benny 11, 45
Gossec, François-Joseph 26
gourd 9
Grand Duo Concertant 31

harp 29
Haydn, Michael 30
Hebrides Overture 35
Herman, Woody 11
Hermstedt, Simon 28, 31, 42, 43
high notes 12, 16
high-pitched clarinets 13
Hindemith, Paul 45
horn 10, 24, 27, 33

India 9
Introduction, Theme, and Variations for
    clarinet and orchestra 33
Italian Symphony 34

jazz 11, 45

Kegelstatt Trio 22
keys 7, 16, 19
keywork 17, 18, 19
Klosé, Hyacinthe Eléonore 15, 43
Koczwara, Frantisek 35

Lefèvre, Jean Xavier 26
Leipzig, Germany 35
ligature 17
London, England 22, 43, 44, 45
low notes 12, 16, 20
low-pitched clarinets 15

Mannheim orchestra 14, 22, 23
Märchenerzählungen 37
Maximilian I of Bavaria, King 31
Meiningen, Duke of 39, 44
Meiningen, Germany 44
Mendelssohn, Felix 7, 34–35, 43
Messiaen, Olivier 10
Meyerbeer, Giacomo 7, 43
military bands 14, 32, 33
mouthpiece 6, 17
Mozart, Leopold 22
Mozart, Wolfgang Amadeus 7, 10,
    22–23, 28, 30, 45
Mühlfeld, Richard 37, 38, 39, 44
Müller, Iwan 6, 14
multiphonics 21
Munich, Germany 30, 31
Musgrave, Thea 45

Napoleonic Wars 32
Neefe, Christian Gottlob 24
Nicholson, Charles 43
nickel silver 18
Nonet 29
Nuremberg, Germany 12

oboe 10, 14, 24, 37, 40
Octet in E 29
opera 32
orchestra 6, 14, 24, 34, 37
orchestration 32

Paris, France 26, 33, 42, 43, 44
Parsifal 40
Phantasiestücke 37
phrasing 21
pianissimo 20
piano 10, 25, 36, 37, 38, 39, 41
pibcorn 8
pipes 8, 9
pitch 6, 13, 16, 19
plastic clarinet 18
pungi 5, 9

Quartet for the End of Time 10
Quintet 29

reamer 19
reed 8, 12, 13, 16, 17
Reger, Joseph 40
Reger, Max 40–41
Rhapsody in Blue 21
Roeser, Valentin 14

Rossini, Gioachino 32–33
Salzburg, Austria 23, 30
Sax, Adolphe 15
scales 21
Scheidler, Dorette 29
Schumann, Clara 36, 37
Schumann, Robert 36–37
Schwarzenberg, Prince von 24
Septet 29
serenades 38
Seville, Spain 44
Silvana 31
Sinfonia Concertante 27
snake charmer's pipe 5, 9
sonata 10
sopranino clarinet 6, 13
soprano clarinet 13
Spain 8
speaker key 16
Spohr, Louis 28–29, 42
staccato 21
Stadler, Anton 22, 23, 42
Stamitz, Carl 10, 42
Stockholm, Sweden 26
Strauss, Richard 7
Stravinsky, Igor 10, 11
string quartet 39
Sveaborg, Finland 26

Tausch, Franz 26
tenon-and-socket joints 17, 18
Thieving Magpie, The 32
Thun, Countess von 25
Thurston, Frederick 44, 45
tone 9
tonguing 20
tremolo 21
Trio for clarinet, cello, and piano 39
tube 13, 16
tuning 14, 17

Variations for clarinet 27
Variazioni a più istrumenti obbligati 32
vibration 16
vibrato 21
Vienna, Austria 23, 42
viola 10, 37, 41
violin 41, 44

Wagner, Richard 40
Wales 8
Weber, Carl Maria von 30–31, 43
Wieck, Friedrich 36
Willman, Thomas Lindsay 14, 43
Wood, Henry 44
Württemberg, King of 30

xiao 9

Zelter, Carl Friedrich 34
zummara 8
Zwickau, Germany 36

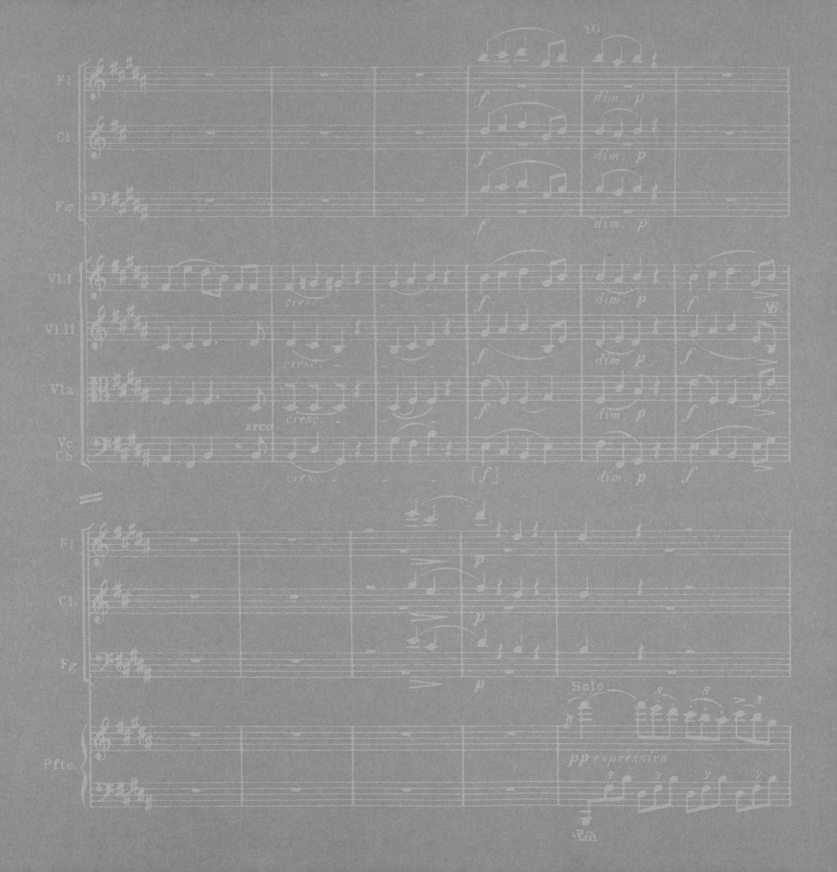